slumberkins®

This book belongs to

Scan here for additional resources and digital
content for Slumberkins' books.

Slumberkins®

PRESENTS

Halloween Fright

By Kelly Oriard with Callie Christensen

Illustrated by Noona Vinogradoff

On Halloween the moon was out,
  a chill held in the air.
The neighborhood was filled with friends,
  looking for a scare.

1.

Kins dressed up in costumes
headed to The Monster Ball.
The greatest party of the year
for creatures big and small.

Unicorn was all dressed up,
   with Black Cat Lynx, her friend.
Uni was feeling nervous,
   as they walked around the bend.

The sounds and sights felt spooky,
   she wished it all would end.
It was hard to remember
   that it was all pretend.

3.

Just then they heard a sound,
giving Unicorn a scare.
"What was that?!" she shrieked,
"I heard it over there!"

AhHOOOO

AhHOOOOO

the sound howled again,
  her legs turned into mush.
Then out popped Werewolf Fox
  from a nearby bush.

5.

Yeti poked her head out, too.
　　She looked just like a mummy!
Unicorn let out a sigh
　　and breathed into her tummy.

"I am so glad it's you, my friends,
　　you gave me quite a scare.
I heard howling in the darkness,
　　and I didn't see you there!"

"We are sorry Unicorn,"
   Fox said with lots of care.
"We were being silly,
   and didn't mean to scare!"

Uni smiled at her friends,
ready to keep going.
"Let's keep heading to the ball,
before the wind starts blowing."

8.

They all traveled down the path
in the moonlight glow,
but it was only Uni,
who saw the dark shadow.

Then swooping from the sky,
came a bat with a toothy grin.

"HEY THERE EVERYBODY! WHAT ARE YOU ALL DOIN'?"

AAAAH!

shrieked Unicorn,

"A bat! Let's hide or run!
I heard that they can bite us
and ruin all our fun."

11.

"Hold on," replied Yeti
with a little nudge.
"Maybe we don't need to fear,
let's not rush to judge."

12.

Bat swooped down beside them,
   still giving them some space.
Looking shy and friendly,
   a sweet look upon his face.

"I do not plan to bite,
   that I promise you.
Can I come along,
   and join the party, too?"

Uni's body softened
  as she heard the creature speak.
"I'm feeling that's okay with me,
  I'm sorry that I shrieked."

14.

"It's no problem Uni,"
said her friendly crew,
"It's normal to be scared
when something startles you."

15.

The group continued on
to see what they could see.
Until Uni began to feel
something sticky in the tree.

"Oh no! What's that I feel?
It's a sticky mess!
It might be a spiderweb,
that is my best guess."

16.

Uni paused and told herself,
  'Spiders aren't so bad.'
Maybe she could meet this one
  and end up feeling glad.

17.

Uni took a breath,
then a spider sweet and small
dropped down from the tree
and asked,

"ARE YOU GOING TO THE BALL?"

"Yes," said all the creatures,
"Would you like to come?
There is room for us all
to join in on the fun!"

18.

The friends walked on together
until they arrived at the ball
and greeted all their pals
to celebrate this fall.

19.

Their other friends, Vlad and Frank,
　met them at the door.
And let them in together,
　where they danced upon the floor.

Unicorn felt proud that night
   as she danced on with her peers.
The worries that she wasn't safe,
   were simply just her fears.

21.

She'd learned to trust her body
   if it wants to run or freeze.
But she also knew to calm her mind
   to put herself at ease.

We all have fears sometimes
that make us want to hide.
But when we realize we are safe,
we can trust it deep inside.

When I'm faced with fear,
    I know where to start.
I make sure I am safe,
    then follow my brave heart.

24.

Reflect & Connect

It's common to try to help children through their fears by dismissing the concern completely. However, this can lead to children not trusting their intuition later on as adults. This story encourages children to trust their instincts when they feel afraid and also to become curious and explore new things when they feel ready to do so.

——— Deepen the Learning ———

(1) What things gave Unicorn a scare on her way to The Monster Ball?

(2) What did Unicorn do to calm her body when she felt scared?

(3) What things make you feel scared? What helps you feel safe?

Adult Engagement: What have you learned about your own intuition? Can you trust it?

slumberkins®

Discover a World of Feelings

From understanding emotions to strengthening their inner voice, give children the tools that support them to be caring, confident, and resilient.

The Caring Crew

IBEX — EMOTIONAL COURAGE · YETI — MINDFULNESS · SLOTH — ROUTINES · OTTER — BUILDING CONNECTION · HONEY BEAR — GRATITUDE

The Confidence Crew

BIGFOOT — SELF-ESTEEM · UNICORN — AUTHENTICITY · HAMMERHEAD — CONFLICT RESOLUTION · NARWHAL — GROWTH MINDSET · YAK — SELF-ACCEPTANCE

The Resilience Crew

FOX — CHANGE · ALPACA — STRESS RELIEF · SPRITE — GRIEF AND LOSS · LYNX — SELF-EXPRESSION · DRAGON — CREATIVITY